My Little Pony™

THE TROLLS AND THE CASTLE OF DARKNESS

THE TROLLS AND THE CASTLE OF DARKNESS

One day, on her way to Dream Castle, Cotton Candy stopped to munch some bluegrass that grew near the waterfall. She paused for a moment to splash Bubbles, who was taking a bath to get rid of the mud that the little pony had rolled in.

Bubbles loved mud, and she loved bubbles even more than Sprinkles and Duck Soup, who were also playing in the waterfall. Bubbles watched Sprinkles turn a back flip and clapped.

Suddenly the ponies heard the sound of footsteps . . . human footsteps! "Someone's coming," whispered Cotton Candy. "Who can it be?"

"It's a young man," said Sprinkles, flying over the treetops to look. "He's wearing a crown! He must be a prince!"

The young man stopped when he saw the ponies. "My name is Prince Valiant," he said. "I am looking for the Castle of Darkness."

PV

"Oh, you mustn't go there, that's where the terrible green trolls live," cried Cotton Candy. "It's a horrible place."

"Yes, I know," said Prince Valiant. "But I must go, for the trolls have captured Princess Rosabelle, the girl I'm going to marry. I must rescue her, no matter what the danger may be!"

"You need help," said Sprinkles. "Come with us to the Dream Castle to see Majesty and the others. We'll think of a plan to rescue the princess."

"Thank you," said the prince, and he followed Sprinkles, Cotton Candy, Duck Soup and Bubbles to the enchanted castle.

As they went inside Prince Valiant heard the sound of happy whinnies

and the clatter of hoofs as the ponies played hide-and-seek around the castle. "We come to lunch at the castle every day," explained Cotton Candy. "Majesty provides molasses, corn and oats for everyone, and then we play games and have lots of fun!"

"But Cotton Candy eats flowers instead," laughed Bubbles with a wicked chuckle. "He's got a sweeter tooth than any bee!"

"Here come Majesty and the others," said Candy. "Majesty, we need your help . . . listen!"

Majesty and the other ponies gathered round while Prince Valiant told them his story.

"Can you use your magic horn to bring the princess here?" asked Lemon Drop.

"No, the trolls have strong magic of their own, and they would use it against me," replied Majesty. "In their castle no one is stronger than they, but once outside . . . Listen, my friends, I have a plan."

Using her magic, Majesty transported all the land ponies across the sky, over the rainbow, through the Gloomy Glade and the Terrible Trees, and into the Frightening Forest where the Castle of Darkness stood.

Seaspray sailed her boat, carrying Prince Valiant, across the ocean so that he reached the Frightening Forest from the other side.

"I shall have to leave you here. Good luck!" cried Seaspray.

"Yes, good luck against the green trolls," echoed Wavebreaker and Surfdancer, who had followed the sailboat.

"Remember, Prince Valiant, once the trolls leave the safety of their

castle, their magic fades. They become as mortal men, they feel pain and fear, just like you."

"I will remember. Thank you, sea ponies, for bringing me so far on my journey," replied Valiant as he set off through the Frightening Forest.

"How dark it is!" he cried as he pushed his way through the trees. "I can scarcely see the way ahead, and the trees have such strange faces . . . they seem to claw at me with their branches as if they are wild animals. Oh, I must not give up and get lost! I will reach my princess, I will, I will!"

"Be of good heart, Valiant," said a voice, which sang:

"I am here to guide your way,
Moondancer is my name.
See how I glow through darkest night,
Let's make the journey like a game.
We'll play hide and seek among the trees.
Come now, don't be afraid,
'Cos Firefly and Medley, too, are here,
They've come to your aid!"

Prince Valiant looked around in astonishment and there he saw a pony with a unicorn horn on her head. A bright light glowed all around her, clearly showing the way ahead. Nearby stood two

ponies. One had musical notes on her body, a green mane and tail, and wings sprouting out of her sides. The other, a pink pony with blue mane and tail, was also winged, with blue flashes of lightning on her body.

"We will show you the way and help you all we can," sang Medley softly.

"I can fly swifter than troll or man," cried Firefly confidently:

"Come, Valiant, cast off your
gloom,
On we go to the castle of doom!
There we'll rescue your
princess,
And bring you both great
happiness."

Filled with hope, Valiant set off with his two pony friends, and soon they reached the middle of the Frightening Forest where the Castle of Darkness stood.

It gleamed with an eerie green light and strange stone figures seemed to guard the entrance.

"How are we going to get inside?" cried the prince. "And look! Hundreds of windows! How will I ever find my princess?"

"Just make a wish and you will be inside," said Majesty, stepping out of the shadows, wearing her royal robe. "Trust me and all will be well!"

Valiant whispered softly, and as he did so Majesty's magic horn granted his wish . . .

"Dear Rosabelle, I have come to rescue you!" cried the prince as he opened his eyes and found himself standing in a room with his bride.

"Oh, Valiant, how can you? The trolls guard every door," protested the princess. "Go, before you are discovered and imprisoned, too!"

"Fear not, our pony friends will help us," promised Valiant. "Just be ready to escape when we can!"

Meanwhile, the trolls were having supper.

Suddenly Topaz, the leader of the trolls, cried for silence.

"Listen, I hear drumbeats," he cried. "The castle is under attack. We must go out and fight."

"Nay, master, if we go out we will lose our power," protested Jade, the captain of the troll guard. "It is a trick to get us outside."

"You may be right, Jade," agreed Topaz. "The drums are fading now . . . but listen to that sweet singing . . . it is like a harp! I must go out! Come, trolls, let us find this wonderful singer . . ."

Drawn by the sweetness of Medley's voice, the trolls left the safety of the castle, and with each step their magic grew weaker until just outside the castle gates . . .

"The first part of our plan is working, the trolls are out of the castle," chuckled Lemon Drop as he stood beside Medley. "They did not think that your hoof beats were soldier's drums, but your sweet voice led them out. Well done, Medley!"

"Aw, pony-feathers," grinned Medley. "Let's hope the other battle plans work!"

"Applejack, Bow-Tie, Bubbles, are you ready?" called Majesty.

"We are all ready, Majesty," called the ponies.

"Start Operation Troll!" ordered Majesty.

As the trolls streamed out into the forest Applejack started to throw apples at them. They were the hardest she could find, and Majesty's magic had turned them even harder . . . as hard as rocks!

"Ouch . . . stop . . . that hurt!" cried Jade. "My head . . . what's happening?"

"We're being shelled by apples!"

shouted Topaz. "Back into the castle, trolls!"

But as they turned to go Bow-Tie and Peachy, Cotton Candy and Lemon Drop tripped them up with ribbons supplied by Bow-Tie.

As the trolls fell down, Spike, Duck Soup and Brandy pushed them into the castle moat which Bubbles had filled with soap!

"Oh, our colour is fading . . . we are becoming . . ." began Topaz.

But he never finished because Majesty sang a little spell song:

"Trolls no longer you shall be,
Turned instead to foam you'll
be.
For ever and ever you shall float
Round and round upon the
moat."

And as they watched the ponies saw all the trolls turn to green foam which bubbled angrily against the walls of the castle.

"The trolls are no more," cried Majesty, as all the ponies cheered loudly. "Sprinkles, fly up and bring the prince and his princess safely out of the castle."

"How can we thank you for all you've done?" cried the prince gratefully as he and his princess

stood in the middle of the circle of ponies. "I could never have freed Princess Rosabelle without your help!"

"Aw . . . pony-feathers!" cried Lemon Drop.

"Apple sauce!" grinned Applejack.

"I like to make my friends' dreams come true," said Majesty.

"And I have another idea. Please let Sunbeam arrange your wedding. She loves giving parties."

"And you must all come as our guests!" cried Princess Rosabelle in delight.

And so, at the wedding of Prince Valiant and Princess Rosabelle, Medley sang the wedding song,

Firefly raced across the sky to make sure that the rainbow appeared to wish the royal couple good fortune, and Glory was their pony maid. Cotton Candy was the flower pony, strewing flowers along the path as the royal couple walked under an archway of pretty ribbons held by Bow-Tie, Peachy, Lemon Drop and Firefly.

Applejack gave them a basket of her juiciest apples as a wedding gift and Bubbles and Sprinkles and Duck Soup turned myriads of bubbles into balloons which floated down on everyone as Majesty helped them with one of her special spells.

Later, Sunbeam provided lots of lovely things to eat and everyone played hide-and-seek in the garden. How Moondancer loved creeping up on her friends and giving them a surprise!

Applejack ate so many apples and Cotton Candy so many flowers that they missed the firework display in the evening. The two little ponies fell fast asleep!

But everyone else watched a shower of stars explode in the sky

and they heard shy little Twilight singing:

"Star bright, star bright,
Royal mortals make a wish
tonight,
And I'll make it all come true,
That's my wedding gift to you!"

And do you know what the princess and the prince wished that night? They wished that the little ponies would always be their friends!

And that was one wish that really *did* come true!

Majesty makes *your* wish come true when you blow out your birthday candles, and if you wish on a star, Twilight will be sure to be listening . . .